RED DWARF™

SPACE CORPS
SURVIVAL
MANUAL

SPACE CORPS
SURVIVAL MANUAL

HOW TO SURVIVE THE UNIVERSE'S MOST DEADLY ENVIRONMENTS

BY COLONEL MIKE 'MAD DOG' O'HAGAN

To Albert Rimmel — thanks for buying my book.

Thanks also for the chocolates and for cleaning my shoes. Also thanks for setting me up on a date with your mother. She's a great little mover, although it was a little cramped in the back of my car. What can I say — thanks for holding the door open.

Your friend,

Mike

MANDARIN

A Mandarin Paperback
THE RED DWARF SURVIVAL MANUAL

First published in Great Britain 1996
by Mandarin Paperbacks
an imprint of Reed International Books Ltd
Michelin House, 81 Fulham Road, London SW3 6RB
and Auckland, Melbourne, Singapore and Toronto

Copyright © Grant Naylor 1996
Written by Paul Alexander
The author has asserted his moral rights

Cover and all Red Dwarf photographs by Mike Vaughan
Star map – Francis Leroy, Biocosmos/SPL

Designed by Blackjacks
Colour reproduction by Scanners

A CIP catalogue record for this title
is available from the British Library

ISBN 0 7493 2374 4

Printed and bound by Jarrold Book Printing Ltd, Norfolk, England

INTRODUCTION
by Mike O'Hagan

Ok, Grunts, listen up. You're in the Space Corps now. Which is why you're going to need this book. You've completed basic training and you're about to be launched into deep space. You thought your best friend was your best friend. Wrong!!! Your best friend is this book, because this book will teach you how to survive. Forget 'civilised' society, now it's 'survival of the fittest'. I have seen many good men and women under my command perish because they lacked the survival instinct. All of them were brave. Most of them were noble. And many of them were simply delicious and filling when accompanied by a simple stew of nettles and berries. They did not have what it takes to survive – have you?

Yes, I've eaten human flesh. I'm not proud of it – but I'm alive. I've also eaten many of my own body parts – and I don't have any regrets. Well…maybe one. Undercooking my appendix. But I did what I had to do. And so must you. This book can help. Read it. Study it. Live it. And, when you're stuck in the middle of the desert in 100 degree temperature, with no water and raging dysentery, I hope you'll enjoy using it just as much as I did writing it.

A bit of mindless violence never hurt anyone.

Mike

ABOUT THE AUTHOR

Mike O'Hagan served as a Space Marine with the Space Corps Special Service Really Really Brave Division (SCSSRRBD) for almost thirty years. Mike has survived over two hundred space crashes and has lived in survival situations for almost half of his adult life. Mike has 459 scars and his nose has been broken so many times he is now able to remove it and travel with it in his pocket.

During his career, Mike has had 12 pieces of metal inserted into various parts of his head. Nothing to do with head injuries – he just fancied it. He is single with over forty tattoos and lists his hobbies as swearing and long-distance spitting. He has never worn aftershave.

Now he shares the secrets of his survival success with all Space Corps personnel: giving advice, setting them survival tasks and inviting them to log their own survival adventures.

BY THE SAME AUTHOR
Charlie Zero Potato
The Star Corps Commando Big Book of Brutality
Kill Your Way Slim

(For Children)
General George and the Gook Invasion
Kill Your Way Slim (3D Magic Eye Version)

CONTENTS

Survivor Crew Ident. List Dave Lister

Hryten

Arnold Rimmer, Second Technician

Kristine Kochanski

Cat

SPACE CORPS
SURVIVAL QUESTIONNAIRE

Name:

Dave Lister

1. In your opinion, what is the first rule of survival?

The best form of defence is attack and the best form of attack is one that doesn't actually involve you.

If it does, then remember lister's second rule of survival - speak softly and carry a bloody big bazookoid.

2. Would you kill to avoid being killed?

Course I would.

 The way I see it, if it comes down to me or him...it's not gonna be me.
   Though, obviously, that's what he's thinking... except to him, he's not 'him', he's 'me'... so in actual fact, it all comes down to 'me' or 'me'. Or possibly 'him' or 'him'... No wonder people shoot first and ask questions later.

3. Can violence ever be justified?

 I'm not sure. I think it was Mahatma Gandhi who said 'he who fights and runs away...is using up valuable running time with all that fighting' ...no, tell a lie, it was Arnold Rimmer.

4. If you could go back in time and murder Adolf Hitler
   as a baby – would you?

No. Because as a baby, I was too short to murder hitler.. If you mean would I go back in time and murder a baby who would grow up to become Adolf Hitler...I'd probably still say 'no'. I still feel guilty for what happened last week when we went back to 1971 and told Julio Iglesias to give up football and go into music

5. Do you believe in censorship?

No. I bel.eve in t... r... un of everyone in a free soci.cy ... uve a vo.e .. m ne i. heard loud and ..ro.. (wit. ... ol.ious .xception of the eur ..isi.n .ong ..ces! .

6. Would you use the words agnostic/atheist/deist/satanist
   to describe yourself?

No.
Try bored / smegging horny / frustrated / desperate.

7. How would you describe your spiritual position?

I sometimes feel really humbled by the great, infinite vastness of space. And look out, across the constellations, into other galaxies, and I think; "somewhere out there, someone is having sex. Bastard!"

8. Would you describe this glass

as being half full – or half empty?

It's not a glass.
It's a picture of a glass.

If it was actually a glass, it wouldn't be half full or half empty - cos I'd have smegging drunk it!!!

9. If there was one thing you could change to make
   life better – what would it be?

> Invent a way that takeways could be
> delivered by fax.
>
> And – make my birthday a national
>   holiday and give everyone in the
> world the preceding 364 days off to
> prepare.

10. What is the purpose of existence?

> To experience everything you can. Remember, life
>   is not a rehearsal. At least I hope it's not.
> I'd hate to have to go through all this
>   crap six times a week and twice on Saturdays.

A survival situation is something you may have no time to prepare for and little way to think your way out of. To simulate these conditions this book contains a number of mental puzzles which each crew member is required to solve in a strict time limit of two minutes.

MENTAL ACUITY SURVIVAL PROBLEM
ONE

To be solved by: Arnold J. Rimmer

PROBLEM:

You are in your quarters when your ship is hit by an asteroid shower, plunges towards the nearest planet and crashes at the bottom of a ravine. The ravine is filling with water from a dam your vessel cracked when it crashed, and your engine rods are badly ruptured and about to blow – you must abandon ship. You have seconds till doomsday – nowhere near enough time to climb from the ravine, and only just enough time to gather a few things from your quarters before you leave the ship.
How do you escape?

SOLUTION:

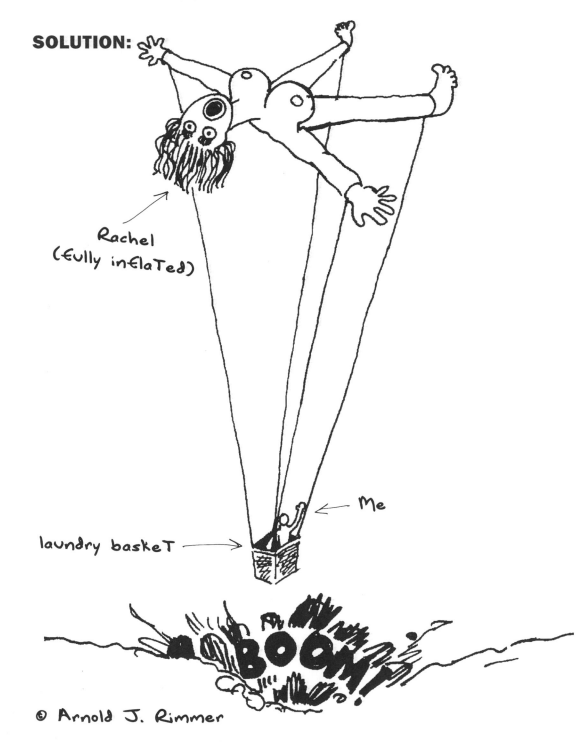

Rachel
(Eully inElaTed)

laundry baskeT →

← Me

© Arnold J. Rimmer

Now Tell me Rachel doesn'T deserve a promoTion.

SOURCES OF FOOD

If you've crash landed on a hostile world, hundreds of thousands of light years from civilisation, one of your first areas of concern (apart from the lack of a video store with the latest blockbuster rental releases) will be to find some food. It's a serious problem, as statistics show that most emergency survival situations occur at least 248,000 light years from earth, while most of earth's Pizza Huts only deliver within a three mile radius. You do the maths.

Assuming you've crashed on a planet with no takeout restaurants (a statistical likelihood), you have three options:

1. STARVE TO DEATH

Inexplicably popular amongst survivors of space crashes. Myself, I've never understood the attraction. It's the most sedentary of the three options, so I suppose appeals to people who don't like exercise. It basically involves large amounts of sitting down and getting thin. Then death. I'd save this one as a last resort, if I were you.

2. EAT YOUR CREWMATES

My personal favourite, and is dealt with in the following pages. The secret is not to think of it as cannibalism, but as recipe-based respect for the dead.

HERE LIES
NIGEL P.
FOWLER

DEVOTED HUSBAND
LOVING FATHER
TASTY RISOTTO

3. FORAGING

If you don't want to eat your crewmates or you're vegetarian (let's face it, most crews don't include even non-commissioned broccoli) then this is your alternative. You will have to find the means to survive on the surface of the planet you crashed on. Success depends largely on the nature of the world you find yourself on. I once went down on an unpopulated planet whose entire surface had been turned over to the cultivation of sweetcorn. But there was no butter so I had to live on a diet of bumble bees and head lice.

Over the last few decades, however, many unpopulated worlds have been 'seeded' with the unwanted or excess results of genetics engineering experiments. Some of these experiments have been well-publicised – creatures such as the duck-billed oyster and the orang-u-rottweiler are now a common sight in our cities. But there are other, more obscure results of the genetic engineers arts you are likely to encounter off-world – and which could well be edible.

For example, gene splicing has given us

THE CHICKANTULA
A cross between a Tarantula and a Rhode Island Red that not only tastes great with sage and onion but means that everyone gets a leg.

THE WILDEBEETROOT
Half mammal, half root-vegetable, great herds of these creatures can be found roaming the plains of planets in the Zsigsmos Sector, so be careful where you locate your campsite. Even in these enlightened times, "trampled to death by beetroot" on the coroner's report can still raise a snigger.

THE WERECOD

An interesting gene-splice this, creating the entirely new species of *lupus aquaticus* – a wolf which provides a filling and nutritious meat dish except on those days of the month when there's a full moon, when it provides a filling and nutritious fish dish. Be careful not to eat this animal just before a full moon rises as having meat stew transmute into bouillabaisse inside your stomach is not a pleasant feeling.

FUTURE DEVELOPMENTS

An exciting development in the world of genetic engineering promises to revolutionise future field survival missions. Scientists say they have isolated the fabled 'doner' gene – the DNA combination that makes kebabs tasty and appetising despite the fact that anyone with half a brain can see they are grey and oily with the texture of a fungal infection.

Within five years, say the boffins, they'll be able to start using that gene to turn ANYTHING into a tasty and irresistible snack-treat (within reason – experts say in the case of the Pot Noodle it will probably only work on certain brands). So on future survival missions we can chow down to doner cactuses, doner athletic supports, doner used cotton buds etc. Bon appetit!

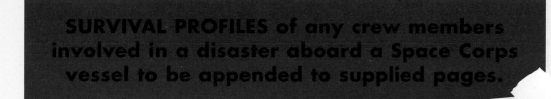

SURVIVAL PROFILES of any crew members involved in a disaster aboard a Space Corps vessel to be appended to supplied pages.

NAME:

Dave Lister

PREVIOUS SURVIVAL EXPERIENCE:

Once went for a whole evening without a curry or a pint of lager. Also once survived several days marooned on an arctic planet with Arnold Rimmer.

SPECIAL SURVIVAL ABILITIES:

Can withstand living conditions that would drive a lesser man insane (ie being marooned on a planet with Arnold Rimmer).

Also – can drink a yard of vindaloo sauce and not die.

SURVIVABILITY RATING:

33% – rising to 96% if he ever crashes on a world whose surface is made from molten korma.

SURVIVAL PROFILE

SELF-CATERING

Should you be stranded on an asteroid, alone, with no sign of sustenance, you will have to face the very real possibility of eating your own body parts.

There is nothing shameful or disgusting about this – just think of it as biting your nails taken to its logical conclusion.

I myself have eaten my own thigh, two knees, a shoulder and a couple of my toes, and it's done me absolutely no harm at all (except for one minor side effect: when I undress for bed, if I catch sight of myself in the mirror, I have to go and make a sandwich).

Here is a beginners guide to eating your own body parts.

1. AFTER THREE DAYS WITHOUT FOOD

Make sure your blade is sharp and that you are wearing a t-shirt (cutting off an arm is no excuse for ruining your uniform).

2. AFTER NINE DAYS WITHOUT FOOD

Don't think of it as losing a limb; think of it as gaining a stew.

3. AFTER 14 DAYS

Remember to amend your Space Corps
members data; your height record
is now inaccurate.

4. ATER 21 DAYS

This stage of the process is the most difficult emotionally, psychologically and, especially, physically, since you won't be able to cook the arm unless you can operate a microwave with your nose.

However, self-service eating is only suggested as a last resort. In a real survival situation you might get lucky – all your friends might be dead! Which brings us to...

CANNIBALISM

Preparing for the death of a friend or loved one is never easy. In a survival situation it is doubly difficult. But here are a few things you should do:

Cut up 3lbs of root vegetables and dice at least one full size onion. Bring a large vat of water to the boil. Boil your friend for at least an hour, stirring at regular intervals, and season to taste.

When it comes to eating people, recipes should be kept simple but delicious. As a pointer, these are the ones I get asked for time and time again...

Bert Bourgignon
Baked Alannah
Steak and Sidney Pie
Billy Con Carne

And remember: **A Friend In Gravy Is A Friend Indeed.**

SURVIVOR DINING TIPS

PLEASE SHARE ANY DINING TIPS YOU HAVE FOUND USEFUL IN SURVIVAL SITUATIONS BELOW

NAME

Arnold Rimmer

TIP

KryTen's pasTry, if TighTly packed in an anTi-aircrafT morTar, has been known To bring down gelf ships.

NAME

Hryten

TIP

Always carry a little minced space weevil in your utility belt. Then – when no one is looking – add it to dishes that are already being cooked. This makes food supplies go further and means Mr Lister doesn't suspect a thing! (NOTE: make sure you don't keep the space weevil in your utility belt for too long, or you will cease being invited to respectable parties).

NAME Dave Lister

....

TIP Every time you order a takeaway curry, save the little bag of salad garnish that comes with it. You'll soon build up quite a collection.

Should you crash, for God's sake don't eat it — it's disgusting — but it makes great bedding material.

NAME

....

TIP

....

....

....

....

....

NAME

....

TIP

....

....

....

NAME

....

TIP

NAME

....

TIP

....

NAME

Kristine Kochanski.

TIP

If you know you're going to be in a
survival situation try and prepare.
Take at least twelve issues of
Vanity Fair and something chic to
wear in the evenings.

NAME

Cat

TIP

When you're really peckish try regurgitating
a fur ball or two. Fried in a little butter
with fresh herbs they can be really tasty.
Also you don't have to share them around.
you'll be amazed how many of your crew
mates will suddenly no longer be hungry.

NAME

TIP

NAME

TIP

SURVIVAL PROFILE

NAME:

Arnold J. Rimmer

PREVIOUS SURVIVAL EXPERIENCE:

Once spent 600 years on a planet with only clones of himself for company. Difficult to know whether to feel more sorry for him or the clones.

SPECIAL SURVIVAL ABILITIES:

Can alphabetize an underwear drawer quicker than anyone else in Space Corps.

SURVIVABILITY RATING:

950%. Unfortunately. (Hard as old nails – but slightly less charismatic).

MENTAL ACUITY SURVIVAL PROBLEM
TWO

To be solved by: Hryten

PROBLEM:

You are faced with a half-crazed simulant who has rewired his internal body-circuitry to turn himself into an enormous 'cussion bomb and is threatening to destroy your ship and anyone on it unless you accede to his demands and turn control of the vessel over to him.

BUT – if you do, you know he will jettison you and the entire crew into deep space anyway.

What do you do?

SOLUTION:

Simply set up a remote microwave transceiver unit to jam his synaptic/servo interface mechanism, locking all override commands in a 'grip o' death', while removing his primary networked processor relays and replacing them with a conically shielded luminescence centre. In layman's terms...

...turn him into an attractive but functional floor lamp.

SNARES AND TRAPS

The flora and fauna of an unknown planet can provide a beautiful and fascinating backdrop to your survival adventure. Many offworld animals are breathtakingly lovely and surprisingly peacable creatures. So why not eat them?

Many can be trapped by using the basic snare, sketched below...

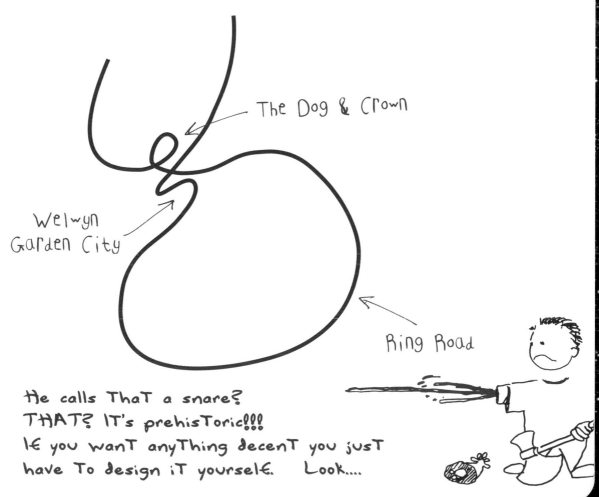

The Dog & Crown

Welwyn Garden City

Ring Road

He calls ThaT a snare?
THAT? IT's prehisToric!!!
If you wanT anyThing decenT you jusT
have To design iT yourself.   Look....

NOTES:

Arnold J Rimmer's InsTanT Dinner Trap
©Arnold J Rimmer

STep 1

Big orange cooking poT wiTh poncey French name

ProjecTed TrajecTory oÆ poT

Flame cannon seT To 25... (1800C wiTh Æan assis... Ælam... Throw...

innocenT birdie

phoToelecTric beam

STep 2

TWEET?

ÆLANG!

NOTES:

STep 3

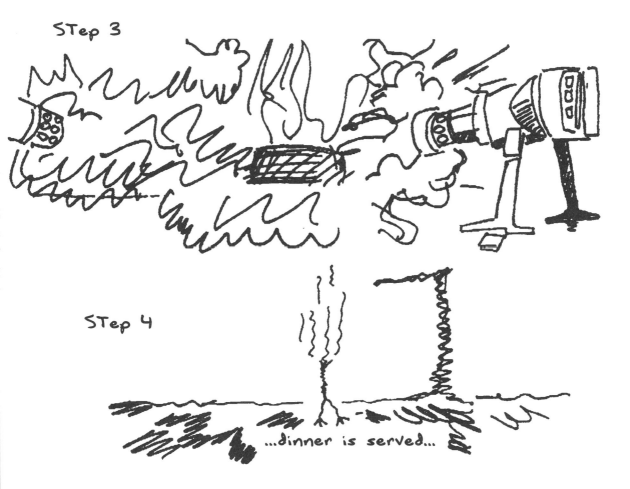

STep 4

...dinner is served...

And where do we get the laser cannons from, Rimmer?

Or the photo electric cell.
 Or the cooking pot.
Rimmer?

Smeg off.

SPACE CORPS
SURVIVAL QUESTIONNAIRE

Name: Cat

1. In your opinion, what is the first rule of survival?

The one that comes immediately before the second rule of survival.

Are you stupid or something??

2. Do you enjoy violent films or vidshows?

Yeah, but that don't make me a violent person. And anyone who says it does gets a knuckle pitta!

3. Would you kill to avoid being killed?

Buddy, I'd kill to avoid wearing polyester!

4. Can violence ever be justi'

Only if you're fighing for something really IMPORTANT – like the last sachet of conditioning rinse.

5. If you could go back in time and murder Adolf Hitler
   as a baby – would you?

yup.

Then I'd go after the guy who invented shell suits.

6. Do you believe in censorship?

No.

But I used to believe in the Tooth fairy.

7. Would you use the words agnostic/atheist/deist/satanist
   to describe yourself?

Maybe.

If I knew what the hell they meant.

8. How would you describe your spiritual position?

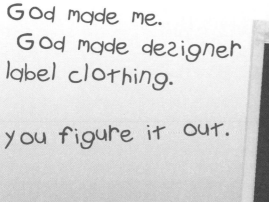

God made me.
 God made designer
label clothing.

you figure it out.

9. Would you describe this glass

as being half full – or half empty?

Sure. One of those.

10. If there was one thing you could change to make
life better – what would it be?

kill the guy who invented shell suits

(see question 5)

11. What is the purpose of existence?

To dream the
impossible dream;
wrinkle-free silk.

APPOINTING A LEADER

In a survival situation, there is always the possibility that your commanding officer will have been lost in the disaster. Perhaps he will have died in an enemy attack, perished trying to pilot your ship to safety, or perhaps – as in the case of my first space disaster – he'll have tripped and hit his head in the rush to get to the grav-chutes before everyone else.

What does it matter – he's dead. You're not. So take his clothes, steal his valuables and then, depending on your mood, eat him, bury him or play hoopla with his genitalia to pass the time until rescue.

With your leader dead your first task is to appoint a new leader.

LEADERSHIP QUALITIES

To identify who among you possesses the most leadership qualities, consider:

- Is there someone who never fetches or carries anything for him/her self?

- Who relies on others to accomplish even the most rudimentary task they could perform themselves?

- Who is quick to find fault with others and equally quick to spring to their own defence at the tiniest of imagined criticisms?

- Who readily takes credit for anything good that happens but whenever anything goes wrong desperately tries to put the blame on YOU?

There is? Then CONGRATULATIONS!!! You've found your leader!

ARE YOU A LEADER?

To assist in the rapid appointment of a new leader in a possible emergency survival situation, readers are requested to list their Leadership Qualities.

NAME Arnold Rimmer

LEADERSHIP QUALITIES

Looks good in uniform.

Already have nice short 'leader' Type haircut.

Have been known To saluTe officers BEFORE They enTer a room.

Do GREAT General PaTTon impression (walk only)

NAME Cat

LEADERSHIP QUALITIES

If dropped from a high place will always land on my feet (unless drunk) - and frequently someone else's.

Can outrun a space weevil.

Will provide own dress uniform.

SPACE CORPS SURVIVAL MANUAL

NAME

. . . .

LEADERSHIP QUALITIES

. . . .

. . . .

. . . .

. . . .

NAME

. . . .

LEADERSHIP Q

. . . .

. . . .

. . . .

. . . .

NAME   Kryten

. . . .

LEADERSHIP QUALITIES

Very good at vacuuming. Superb ironer.
Uh, that's it....

No, wait. Have commanded an army of 3 skutters
(who voted me "mech most likely to be
mutineered against")

NAME

Kristine Kochanski

LEADERSHIP QUALITIES

* Understanding, empathy

* Recognising that each and every soldier is actually a person and must be communicated with as such rather than as a fighting machine

* Can live without make-up for up to three days in the wild

NAME

Dave Lister

LEADERSHIP QUALITIES

Can drink twelve pints, two rum chasers, eat four bags of crisps and a mixed tandoori special and not throw up on anyone on the way home.

NAME

LEADERSHIP QUALITIES

LEADERSHIP RESPONSIBILITIES

The team leader shoulders the three basic responsibilities of command:

TEAM MORALE, TEAM WELLBEING and **TEAM DISCIPLINE**

MORALE

Your ship has disintegrated, smashed into the surface of a blazing hellhole – a planet with 15 suns and no water, populated by flesh-eating giant mutant lizards. Try and see the funny side.

<u>TRY TO KEEP CHEERFUL</u>

There's nothing worse than being in a desperate, life or death situation surrounded by long faces. The leader is responsible for putting a smile – or at the very least, a rictus grin – on the faces of his troops. The leader's job is to keep spirits up, and to remind his troops that no disaster seems as bad, no tragedy as tragic, once the survivors have gathered round the campfire for a few verses of 'Achy Breakey Heart'.

Another good tip for easing the psychological trauma of a disaster is to take a good look around the immediate area your ship has smashed into. As you look at the charred remnants of your ship and crew, try not to think of it as a crash site. Think of it as a theme park. You're surrounded by fascinating and appealing bits of both your ship and your former colleagues. Why not use them to stage some fun and morale-boosting party games?

Below are a few of the favourites I've developed over my last dozen or so fatal missions (©Mad Mike O'Hagan 2347)

- PIN THE NOSE ON THE CRASH VICTIM
- MUSICAL RUBBLE
- PASS THE PART
- RING AROUND THE IMPACT CRATER
- KISS CHASE (not advisable among all male crews. Before you know it, they'll be humming Broadway shows and criticising your haircut)
- BOBBING FOR ADAMS APPLES

After a fun evening playing the above games, you'll have even the most tired and ravenous crewmembers eating out of your hand (note the words 'out of'. They're important).

WELL BEING

A leader should treat his troops like his family: forget their birthdays and keep telling them they were much nicer when they were little.

DISCIPLINE

Discipline means different things to different people. To some, it might mean homework, to others a diet, while to still others among us, it means two Swedish twins who wear a lot of leather.

But let me make it quite clear what discipline means in the survival context. It means FOLLOWING ORDERS. Without hesitation. Without question. Without thinking. For, just as the body has only one brain (except in the case of Breakfast TV presenters, where this is admittedly a tad optimistic) so the team can only have one leader. Everyone on the team is subservient to his will and should he tell them all to take off their clothes, form a human pyramid and set fire to their armpit hair then they must assume he has a perfectly good reason for doing so and obey without question. As my survival team of '49 did, incidentally. (Funny story – I actually didn't have any good reason; I'd just eaten a hallucinogenic mushroom by mistake!!!!)

Without discipline we have anarchy. And who wants that? Well, anarchists, obviously. But apart from them – who wants that? Not me. And not you. Which is why in a survival situation you will have to learn to obey your leader. It is up to the leader not to abuse this position of trust. Discipline must be used wisely. For instance, it is not necessary to have a man put to death just for 'looking at you funny'. A simple beating is sufficient. Firmness must be tempered with kindness.

Below is a list of what I have found the most common signs of insubordination – together with the minimum necessary response to deal with them.

- 'Looked at me funny' – brutal beating.

- 'Called me "sir" in a really, really sarcastic tone' – shot.

- 'Saluted in a disrespectful manner' – shot and quartered.

- 'After listening to my plan said "Right!" then made weird braying sound with his lips' – shot. Family hunted down and killed.

- 'Called me a cross-dressing, psychotic Fascist nutball' – sent to bed without supper.

HARD CHOICES

As leader you have certain responsibilities which cannot be shirked. In order to survive you will have to make tough decisions, and you'll have to make them quickly – 'Procrastination is the Enemy of the True Warrior', as it'll say on the sign I've been meaning to put up in my office for the past couple of years.

Harder still, you will have to take every decision based on what you perceive as the 'common good', rather than on personal preferences or your own individual sense of what's right or wrong. This can be a burden. I still vividly remember the time on Altair when I had to have my best friend shot for stealing the operation codes of our All Terrain Land Vehicle – a doubly horrible moment as while they were burying him I found I actually had them in my other trousers.

Still, I made the right decision based on the information available to me at the time. And so must you! Always remember – the needs of the many outweigh the needs of the few or the one...unless of course, the few or the one need really HEAVY things and the many only need light stuff, like tissues or feather dusters. Then the needs of the few might outweigh the needs of the many... bugger.
Lost my train of thought.

THE NEEDS OF THE MANY

In certain survival situations, the common good dictates that you abandon survivors who are sick or old in order to more easily ensure the safe passage of the rest.*

*Unless you yourself are sick or old in which case the aged and infirm must naturally be treated with the dignity and care they have a right to expect.

No matter how heartless or cruel it may seem, you have no right to jeopardise the safety of the survivors relying on you by getting sentimental about a few old codgers or a handful of people whingeing on about how their internal bleeding hurts.

Sick people are easy to spot and will normally be too weak to object when you dump them. The elderly are a different story. Thanks to modern plastic surgery and toupee-thatching techniques, it can actually be quite difficult to tell that someone IS old until it's too late and you're in the middle of fleeing from some ferocious flesh-eating mutant with some irritating old scroat whingeing on about how it must be time to stop off for a toilet break. However, there are certain tell-tale signs you can look out for to identify the elderly, and get shot of them before they get too irritating.
A survivor is almost certainly too old to go on if he or she:

- Keeps pointing at everything and saying they can remember when all this was grass.

- Carries round an autographed photo of Joan of Arc in their wallet

- Are told they can save one thing of value to them from the crash-site – so they bring a shopping bag with little wheels on it.

- Attends a kit inspection wearing furry tartan slippers.

- Gets great radio reception on his/her new hip.

NAME:

Kryten

SURVIVAL PROFILE

PREVIOUS SURVIVAL EXPERIENCE:

Survived for several centuries among the wreckage of the Nova 5 and its dead crew. Was relieved to be rescued however as the situation had become desperate – he was down to his last hoover bag.

SPECIAL SURVIVAL ABILITIES:

Can create tasty yet slimming salads out of most available flora

SURVIVABILITY RATING:

147%. Unless wearing Spare Head Two, in which case – 2%

SPACE CORPS
SURVIVAL QUESTIONNAIRE

Name:

> Arnold J. Rimmer

1. In your opinion, what is the first rule of survival?

> Never Tell a Hell's angel one of his TaTToos is misspelled (I speak from personal experience)

2. Do you enjoy violent films or vidshows?

> If The violence is being used inTelligenTly – as a meTaphor for The ills of socieTy, perhaps – Then yes. I will waTch.
> BuT if iT is graTuiTous and Tacked on for cheap commercial reasons Then I absoluTely will NOT. Unless The women's gymnasTics has finished on The oTher side.

3. Would you kill to avoid being killed?

If iT was me or The oTher guy. Or, preferably, girl. Girl midgeT. Yes, if iT was me or The oTher wheelchair bound dwarf-girl – you beTcha. AbsoluTely. WiThouT mercy.

Er...I would have a weapon, wouldn'T I?

4. Can violence ever be justified?

Every Time LisTer geTs his guiTar ouT.

5. If you could go back in time and murder Adolf Hitler
   as a baby – would you?

An inTriguing eThical dilemma which Throws up all manner of moral quesTions. Is evil inherenT in us? Can a baby be considered 'evil' or does he acquire iT? NaTure or nurTure? Is man sainT or sinner? And The mosT imporTanT quesTion of all – would I have a weapon? A big one???

6. Do you believe in censorship?

Censorship is an insidious blighT on our glorious democraTic Freedoms and anyone who advocaTes iT is dangerous and should be silenced and all Their wriTings burned.

7. Would you use the words agnostic/atheist/deist/satanist
   to describe yourself?

AcTually, I'm a ChrisTian ScienTisT.
I dissecT archbishops.

(ThaT was a JOKE, in case God's reading This...)

8. How would you describe your spiritual position?

I'm a lapsed agnosTic. I believe in God.

I'm jusT noT sure I TrusT Him.

9. Would you describe this glass

as being half full – or half empty?

If ThaT's a red, iT shouldn'T even BE in ThaT
glass. IT should be in a wine glass. And I hope
you decanTed iT properly. I Think I see
sedimenT aT The boTTom. Is iT The '69?

10. If there was one thing you could change to make
    life better – what would it be?

LisTer's underpanTs.

11. What is the purpose of existence?

PoinTing ouT every single one of people's
sTupid liTTle misTakes.

And Trying To be popular...

MENTAL ACUITY SURVIVAL PROBLEM
THREE

To be solved by: DAVE LISTER

PROBLEM:

A group of transtemporal terrorists have captured you, Sir Isaac Newton and Albert Einstein and are holding you as hostages. However, they've just decided they only need one of you and cannot decide which one it should be. You have just 45 seconds to prove your superiority over Einstein and Newton. How do you do it?

SOLUTION:

Challenge them to drink a yard of Vindaloo sauce...

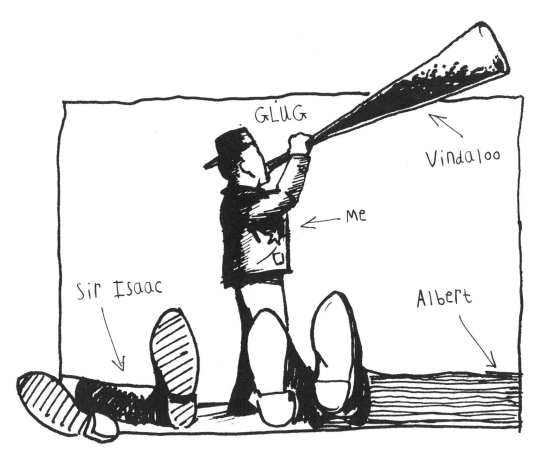

CLIMATE AND TERRAIN

CHOOSING A CAMPSITE

This is very important. Always pick somewhere not liable to flooding, in the shelter of trees and ideally a short walk from a top notch hotel. Also be practical: if you have crashed on an arctic planet 180,000 light years from earth during its rainy season, there's absolutely no use choosing a campsite in Benidorm.

DESERT PLANET SURVIVAL

During sandstorms, you should lie on your side with your back to the wind, cover your face and sleep through the storm.
(Don't worry – you won't get buried. And a bonus is, if you sleep naked, you'll wake up minus your cellulite.)

Me, after discovering The 18 hole golf course was a mirage. Bloody desert survival!

Objects always appear closer than they really are in the desert. Therefore, multiply all your measurement estimations by three (unless you're an estate agent, in which case you should simply reduce them by two).

Also remember the number one rule of those masters of desert survival, the French Foreign Legion: your camel is a fellow officer and will not appreciate unwelcome sexual advances.

ARCTIC PLANET SURVIVAL

An officer's survival chances in the arctic will depend on rank. A general with four stars will last longer in freezing conditions than a general with three stars (as well as generals, this also applies to fishfingers).

In sub-zero conditions after spending 6 hours in a high wind building an igloo, do not seek a cheap laugh by saying 'anyone fancy a choc-ice?'

kochanski demonstrating
a) a sub-zero survival
   outfit,
or
b) her impression of a
sleeping bag.

WATER

Water can be detected by atmospheric conditions, the marshiness of the soil and by the behaviour of local birds and animals. You can be certain of the presence of water if you observe a bird doing these things:

1. Flying straight and low
2. Flying from tree to tree

3. The breaststroke

After you've been in the survival game as long as me and those of my colleagues who are still breathing, you start to develop a 'sixth sense' about what is edible and what is not, no matter what type of world you are on.

SURVIVAL PROFILE

NAME:
Kristine Kochanski

PREVIOUS SURVIVAL EXPERIENCE:
Limited. As a child was left on her own in Boots for half an hour.

SPECIAL SURVIVAL ABILITIES:
Ace cartographer; annoy her and not only will she tell you where to go – she'll draw you a map.

SURVIVABILITY RATING:
62% – and higher among pharmacists.

LOST AT SEA

On returning to Earth your engines pack up during re-entry into the atmosphere and you're forced to crash land in the ocean. What do you do?

(figure 1 – sea)

WHICH OCEAN?

There are lots of different seas, lakes and oceans on the planet Earth; if you really must crash try and find a warm one.

Best ocean: Indian Ocean – warm, full of fish, lots of topless bathing. Worst ocean: Arctic Ocean – not quite so warm, topless bathing very rare.

HOW TO SURVIVE AT SEA

STEP ONE.

The first part of surviving at sea is being first out of the craft before it sinks.

General safety procedure dictates that you shouldn't panic, shout or scream, but disembark in an orderly fashion from your craft.

THIS IS WRONG

Panicking and screaming hysterically is an excellent technique to get to the front of the queue. Baying like a mating stag is also another first class strategy to make people stand aside and let you through. It is also generally acknowledged that you should NEVER inflate your life jacket whilst on board.

THIS IS ALSO WRONG

An inflated life jacket is absolutely excellent for barging people out of the way as you make your stag-baying pelt towards the Exit.

ON HITTING THE WATER

The first rule on hitting the water is: don't drown. This is such a simple rule but you'd be amazed at how many non-swimmers simply ignore it.

ATTRACTING ATTENTION

Raise one arm in the air and move from side to side.

(figure 2 – typical wave)

<u>THIS TECHNIQUE NEVER WORKS BUT LOOKS FUNNY.</u>

SPACE CORPS SURVIVAL MANUAL

Warning: In my experience crew members cast adrift at sea with really big bottoms will find it almost impossible to climb into dinghies if the sea is choppy. You can put this inability to good use. For example; don't waste time trying to rescue them. Instead harpoon them and put their big butts to nutritious use. After all survival is the name of the game.

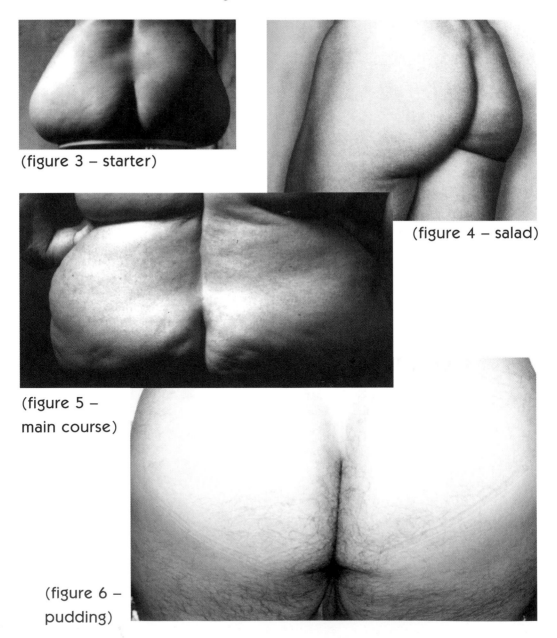

(figure 3 – starter)

(figure 4 – salad)

(figure 5 – main course)

(figure 6 – pudding)

Advice 1. Don't have a big butt.

Advice 2. If you're about to crash land in the ocean, while your other crew mates are panicking, take a quick look around at the size of their butts. Once you've found a real lard arse, strike up a conversation with them and become their friend. They will be really grateful.

Warning:

1) Never stare at their bots and lick your lips.
2) Never talk about different bottom recipes within their hearing range.

COOKING IN THE SEA

As your craft crashes into the sea there will almost certainly be oil spillages. Take a lighter in a waterproof box and you can turn these oil spillages into an excellent improvised barbecue.

(figure 7 – improvised barbecue)

WATER RATIONS

If you have no water it is important that you have a very strict rationing system. The following is a rationing system that can keep you going for up to nine days **without any** water.

Day One: No water required. Presumably you've already had something to drink today and the body doesn't need anything for quite some time yet. Promise yourself you'll have something to drink tomorrow.

Day Two: No water required. You have the fun and excitement of the crash to talk about. If you feel thirsty this should act as a good distraction. Promise yourself you'll have something to drink tomorrow.

Day Three: Keep talking about the crash – when you're bored with this, talk about the possibility of shark attack, this should soon get rid of your thirst obsession. Promise yourself you'll have something to drink tomorrow.

Day Four: No, not today – tomorrow, definitely tomorrow.

Day Five: Tell yourself you never said, "definitely tomorrow". You
              must have misheard yourself.

Day Six: Tell yourself today is definitely the day to establish a
              proper water rationing timetable. First drink tomorrow.

Day Seven: Trick yourself into thinking you've just had a drink and
              your thirst obsession has given you temporary amnesia.

Day Eight: Promise yourself if you don't have a drink today you can
              have two drinks tomorrow.

Day Nine: Of the sea!!

Day Ten: Die of thirst.

SHARK ATTACK

It's important to get things into perspective. This isn't the movies
and the truth is very few shark attacks are reported by crash
victims. This is because nearly all of them have been eaten.

HOW TO AVOID DANGEROUS FISH

It might sound a bit like bolting the stable door after the horse has bolted, but the best thing to do to avoid dangerous fish would have been not to have crashed into a shark infested ocean in the first place, wouldn't it? Well, wouldn't it? Yes, it would. But you have haven't you? Not clever, not clever at all.

Let's take a look at the overall picture; your ship has crashed, you're adrift in some ocean, probably cold, lost and miserable, and to top it all some ferocious great fish is now trying to eat you. Is being eaten so bad?

Maybe not.

What the hell else have you got going for you?

This shark might be doing you the biggest favour of your life. I mean, being bitten in half by a shark – is it really so bad? Does it really hurt? At first maybe. Obviously there'll be the initial little tweak or so as it crunches through the bone and skin tissue of your lower abdomen, but how long will that last – twenty, thirty seconds? And then that's it. Your problems are over. Think about it.

I'VE THOUGHT ABOUT IT AND I STILL DON'T WANT TO DIE

You've crash landed in the sea and now you're surrounded by sharks. Don't do anything that will give your position away. Sharks can detect blood, vomit and excrement. Therefore it is vital you throw your excrement as far from you as possible. What are the best throwing techniques: the discus 360 degree spin, or the well aimed skimmer?

<u>NEITHER</u>

The best technique is to make a paper plane and catch a warm air current. In this way your excrement can travel for miles in safety and comfort – keeping you safe from attack.

Warning: Do not tell your fellow survivors about this technique for transporting excrement. It frequently causes bouts of vomiting.

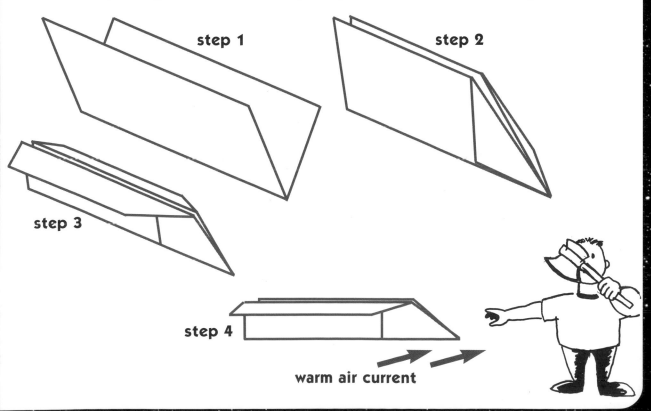

step 1

step 2

step 3

step 4

warm air current

SURVIVAL PROFILE

NAME:

Cat

PREVIOUS SURVIVAL EXPERIENCE:

Once went an entire week without changing his hairstyle.

SPECIAL SURVIVAL ABILITIES:

Sense of smell so acute that he can pinpoint the last time you had a bath to within 15 minutes (in Lister's case – 15 days, which is even more impressive).

SURVIVABILITY RATING:

24% x 9 lives = 216%

SURVIVAL PSYCHOLOGY

If you're like me, you'll find being stranded on a world that wants to kill you, with most of your crewmates dead, incredibly exciting. What I always say is: it's better than sex, 'cos my ex-girlfriend almost never ends up sobbing with frustration after a survival expedition.

However, sadly, some people actually experience negative emotions when faced with near certain death. In my opinion, these people are misguided. Undisciplined. And almost certainly pansies. If you are one of these people – I'm not saying you deserve to perish in a force 15 ion storm, but don't expect me to send a wreath to your funeral.

All right. With that said, my publishers have insisted on a few words about the psychological approach you'll need to take to survive. So here it is.

MENTAL AND PHYSICAL STRESSES

There are several common stresses which prey on both body and mind after you have crashed/been forced to bail out of a starship. They are:

- sense of loss
- pain
- hunger and thirst
- sleep deprivation
- overwhelming feelings of boredom and hopelessness

Certainty I left the iron on.

Conviction that I forgot to set the video to record 'Androids'.

Depressing suspicion that my survival tie clashes with my survival waistcoat and survival spats.

THE SURVIVOR'S MENTALITY

If you have crashed, if all your buddies have been killed, and their dismembered corpses scattered across the terrain like so much confetti, you may be distraught. You may be in pain, experiencing immense mental anguish. But, through all that pain, let your mind fasten onto one, simple thought. A thought that has helped me countless times through moments of crisis. It is this:

<u>ONLY BIG NANCIES CRY IN FRONT OF THEIR MATES</u>

See? Feeling better already, eh? This psychology stuff is not as difficult as all those four-eyed pansies with fancy qualifications make out!

WILL TO SURVIVE

There is one thing that separates man from the beasts that run and slither through the forest – and that is his mastery of semi-automatic weapons. Oh, all right – two things. The other one is his will to survive. According to zoologists, man is amongst the physically scrawniest and least fearsome creatures on God's earth (author excluded obviously). That's right, grunts – <u>you</u> belong to a species that can barely arm-wrestle a chihuahua. But the thing that gives us that special edge, that little something extra (apart from our mastery of semi-automatic weapons) is our will and our wits. You are cunning. You are resourceful. Hell, some of you can obviously even read. You are the masters of your own fate. And so, every morning, I want you to get up and I want you to say "Today I am going to live!" And I want you to say "Today I am going to live" each and every day till the day you die. And on that day, consider this – you failed, LOSER!!!!

Below are some other popular psychological survival techniques.

VISUALISATION

One thing that may help is if you look round at your fellow survivors – and try to imagine them in their underwear (note: this actually may be a technique to help out during job interviews – I'm not quite sure).

THE HAPPY PLACE

We each of us have a happy place. A place in our lives where and when we felt particularly happy or at peace. For some of us it is the sun-dappled meadows of our childhood. For others, the golden sands of a favourite beach. While for others it's a small flat in Ealing occupied by those Swedish twins who dress completely in leather. Wherever it is is, we should always carry a happy place inside us. It's where the child inside lives with his parents inside, both holding down steady jobs to pay the mortgage inside...I'm sorry, can I just say I think this is all bollocks? Can't I just get onto the chapter on eyeball-gouging? Okay, okay...you're the publishers, goddammit... but I would like to point out that I spent £18,000 on three years therapy getting in touch with my child inside. And when I did he asked me to put him up for adoption.

SPACE CORPS
SURVIVAL QUESTIONNAIRE

Name:

> Hryten

1. In your opinion, what is the first rule of survival?

> Early to recharge, early to unplug,
> makes a mech healthy, happy and
> too darn smug.

2. Do you enjoy violent films or vidshows?

If you mean the ones which relish depicting eye gouging, limb chopping, multiple gunshot entry wounds with blood gouting everywhere in an orgy of balletic mayhem, machete decapitations and brutal groin-kicking and face smashing with appropriate crunching, wrenching and slurping sound effects, then - no. I never watch them.

3. Would you kill to avoid being killed?

> I am prevented by my programming from doing such a thing. However my programming does specifically enable me to inflict harm on anyone attempting to hurt fellow members of my crew. Or anyone using the words 'mega', 'wicked' or 'crucial' as an exclamation.

4. Can violence ever be justified?

> No. But ask me again after Mr Rimmer gives his slide lecture on 'The Evolution of the Telegraph Pole 1874-2036'.

5. If you could go back in time and murder Adolf Hitler as a baby – would you?

Sadly, my programming would prevent this. However, I would be prepared to go back and give him a darn good talking to.

6. Do you believe in censorship?

No. Free expression is a vital method of maintaining one's mental fitness. In any situation, you should be able to express yourself freely and tell anyone EXACTLY what you think of them – provided you do it politely, call them 'sir' and offer to iron their socks afterward.

7. Would you use the words agnostic/atheist/deist/satanist to describe yourself?

I more frequently use the words 'precision engineered'.

8. How would you describe your spiritual position?

Please see photo (attached)

9. Would you describe this glass

as being half full – or half empty?

I'd describe it as a silicon based refractive object.

AND I'd do something about that chip in the rim. It's like a holiday camp for germs!

10. If there was one thing you could change to make
    life better – what would it be?

    Upgrade my groinal attachment.

11. What is the purpose of existe

    Life, liberty and the
    pursuit of a larger
    groinal attachment.

MENTAL ACUITY SURVIVAL PROBLEM
FOUR

To be solved by: Arnold J. Rimmer

PROBLEM:

You are on earth's moon, visiting Star Corps headquarters to pick up your monthly expenses. While you are there, the moon is attacked by a Gelf Invasion Fleet. You are the only survivor. As the fleet moves on, you manage to patch a signal through to earth. You have seconds to warn them – to suggest a strategy that will enable them to fight back. The fate of the entire world rests in your hands.

What do you say?

SOLUTION:

I am a fish. I am a fish. I am a fish. I am a fish.
I am a fish. I am a fish. I am a fish. I am a fish.
I am a fish I am a fish I am a fish I am a fish.
I am a fish. I am a fish. I am a fish. I am a fish.
I am a fish. I am a fish. I am a fish. I am a fish.
I am a fish I am a fish I am a fish. I am a fish.
I am a fish. I am a fish. I am a fish. I am a fish.
I am a fish. I am a fish. I am a fish. I am a fish
I am a fish I am a fish. I am a fish. I am a fish.
I am a fish. I am a fish. I am a fish. I am a fish.
   I am a fish. I am a fish. I am a fish I am a fish
     I am a fish. I am a fish. I am a fish. I am a fish.
I am a fish. I am a fish. I am a fish. I am a fish.
I am a fish. I am a fish I am a fish I am a fish.
I am a fish. I am a fish. I am a fish. I am a fish.
I am a fish. I am a fish. I am a fish. I am a fish.
   I am a fish I am a fish I am a fish. I am a fish.
I am a fish. I am a fish. I am a fish. I am a fish.
 I am a fish. I am a fish. I am a fish. I am a fish
I am a fish I am a fish. I am a fish. I am a fish.
I am a fish. I am a fish. I am a fish. I am a fish.
I am a fish. I am a fish. I am a fish I am a fish
 I am a fish. I am a fish. I am a fish. I am a fish.
I am a fish. I am a fish. I am a fish. I am a fish.
  I am a fish. I am a fish I am a fish I am a fish.
I am a fish. I am a fish. I am a fish. I am a fish.
 I am a fish. I am a fish. I am a fish. I am a fish.
 I am a fish I am a fish I am a fish. I am a fish.
I am a fish. I am a fish. I am a fish. I am

SURVIVAL FIRST AID

It may involve eating revolting food out of doors with flesh-biting insects crawling up your trouser legs, but surviving in the wild is no picnic. You'll need at least a working knowledge of survival first aid, diseases, splints and field dressings.

Hey! I ain't getting dressed in no field! Where will I hang my mirror?

CHOKING

These are the most common indicators that a person is choking;

- Person holds his or her throat.
- Person unable to speak.
- Wheezing sounds.

• Person borrows your pen Then hands you a noTe which reads
'Help – I Think I am choking.'

AT leasT ThaT's whaT happened when I was in The Red DwarE canTeen once and a bloke on The nexT Table sTarTed To choke.

ThaT's when I perEormed The Heimlich maneoevre.

THE HEIMLICH MANOEVRE

Kneel or stand behind choking person with your arms round them. Clench one hand over the other, fist pressed thumbside between waist and bottom rib. Press and jerk quickly upwards 4 times.

Wow! Is that what you did to the dude in the restaurant?

No. I always ThoughT The Heimlich manoeuvre was The one where you puT Their head beTween Their legs and made Them drink conTinuous glasses of waTer.

You smeghead! What happened to the guy in the canteen?

He drowned.

SNAKE BITES

Ah yes, snake biTes. Very ~~common~~ RARE!!! in The wild.

Contrary to what you may have been told, the chances of any of your group being bitten by a venomous snake are very small. Nevertheless, it can happen – and if it does, it's definitely worth catching. A venom death is one of the most entertaining deaths you can witness.

NATURAL MEDICINE

Don't think of the horrible, deadly planet where you have crashed as a bad place. Think of it as nature's pharmacy. All around you are things that can help you treat a wide variety of ailments.

- For example – try swallowing charcoal if you have dysentery.

    Or if you're inviTed To one of LisTer's barbecues. I guaranTee iT'll TasTe beTTer Than The food.

- Another way to treat dysentery is to boil tree bark for 12 hours or more. The resulting substance will cure you – though admittedly it'll be black, gooey and smell awful.

    Which is where we get the phrase - his bark is worse than his shite.

- If you have worms, drink a small amount of petrol.

    I've heard this is also a good treatment for haemorrhoids.

    Really, sir?

    Yeah! If you're lucky you can get up to 200 piles to the gallon.

    Very amusing, sir.

- Also remember that maggots can be used to clean a wound.

    Remember when I tried that technique on you on Chakos XII, sir?

    I remember that it wasn't entirely succesful, krytes...

    No sir. Well, it was very difficult trying to get a little bit of Germolene onto the head of each of 48,000 maggots.

SURVIVAL ABOARD SHIP

In certain rare cases when your ship goes down on another planet it may sometimes be more advisable to stay on board ship to await rescue (for example, the planet has an unbreathable atmosphere, a hostile gelf population or a dearth of imitation French bar/cafés).

YOU MIGHT CONSIDER REMAINING ABOARD IF:

1 your ship hasn't disintegrated in the disaster
2 your ship can still pick up the 24-hour Football Channel
3 your ship hasn't been irradiated with a fatal dose of gamma radiation (admittedly this eventuality is so unlikely as to be almost not worth mentioning, as it would actually require the removal of a drive plate by someone then too lazy or too incompetent to replace it properly – and no one's that big a moron).

> *Paging Mr Rimmer...*
> *Smeg OFF!*

If you do decide to forsake the bracing call of the wild for the namby-pamby comforts of remaining with your ship, please bear in mind that all Star Corps vessels come equipped with an expandable biosphere – a completely self-sufficient, self-assembling dome that takes only 12 minutes to set up with enough self-regenerating food, heat and water supplies to sustain up to 4 people in comfort for 900 years.

> *SAY WHAT?!!?*

This is excepting early registration Starbugs, which have a pillow.

> *Typical! Thank you Space Corps!!!*

SURVIVING A/R

Deep Space missions are dull. Imagine being stuck at the monumentally tedious reception of a wedding you didn't want to go to in the first place, talking to someone you hoped you'd never see again halfway through a 3 hour monologue about how he did his own conveyancing. Multiply by 1003. That's a Deep Space mission. If they were any more boring they'd have Polish subtitles.

If you're on one, you need something to break the monotony. Some people collect stamps. Some people get disgusting and inappropriate parts of their bodies pierced. And the real sad gits get so bored that they lose all sense of reason and become rabid 'Risk' enthusiasts.

I resenT ThaT

Whatever else they do, nearly everyone on DS duty will use the onboard Artificial Reality simulator – enabling them to enjoy a diverse and exciting variety of experiences, from wetbiking down the Nile with Cleopatra to bringing law to a lawless town in the Old West, to – my personal favourite – digging a naked supermodel out of a pit of 'quickjello' (raspberry flavour) with their bare hands.

Many of you may have heard tales, perhaps even seen episodes of irresponsible so-called science fictions shows, of how A/R machines suffer from persistent glitches, viruses and design faults which frequently cause dangerous, deadly, even fatal malfunctions.

Of course, that's all fiction.

Real life is much, much worse.

Let's face it – A/R machines go wrong. According to recent figures, there has been a 27% rise in A/R-related deaths. Thanks to a flaw in the binary coding of their respective programs, last May alone saw 329 people die when Captain Horatio Hornblower exploded, 584 perish when Winnie the Pooh went on a rampage with an AK47 and 29,000 unfortunate individuals (mostly men) crushed to death between Betty Boop and Gina Lollobrigida.

Technology isn't perfect. Smeg happens. And it happens quite often in A/R. To stop it happening to you, here are a guide to the most common A/R system malfunctions – and the most popular workarounds.

RETURN TO THE PLANET OF THE CHEERLEADERS

what's meant to happen:
a non-stop sexual marathon that leaves you exhausted and yet strangely satisfied.

most common malfunction:
cheerleaders transmute into a deadly race of killer pom-poms and devour you (and not in a good way).

workaround:
During the Wembley game scene, hop backwards on one leg french-kissing a mongoose while mooning at the royal box. This cheat will immediately take you to the post-coital portion of the program, avoiding the fatal bit. True, the whole point of the game will be ruined – but at least you can have a cigarette.

HAYZE

what's meant to happen:

you enter the beautiful and mysterious land of Hayze, where you progress to the Eye of Serenity through solving an interlocking series of profoundly irritating puzzles.

most common malfunction:

as soon as you arrive, a concert piano falls on you from 2500 feet.

workaround:

as you arrive in Hayze, start singing "Mandy, you came and you gave without taking". Then nothing musical is able to come near you.

SCRAMBLE!!!

what's meant to happen:
you are the pilot of a supersonic Warbird on a daring mission to bomb a simulant munitions dump.

most common malfunction:
you actually find yourself driving a number 17 bus down Balham High Street during the rush hour.

workaround:
you can always bomb Freeman Hardy Willis

A/R USERS!
PLEASE LOG YOUR OWN EXPERIENCE OF PERSISTENT
A/R GLITCHES BELOW (state name and rank):

Rimmer, Arnold J. (Second Technician)
There's a serious problem in 'STraTegic Sea BaTTles'.
 The average punTer probably wouldn'T recognise iT,
buT as I'm a biT of a miliTary hisTorian, I know for a
facT ThaT aT The BaTTle of Trafalgar, The English
were noT lead To a glorious vicTory over The invading
        French fleeT by a dolphin named 'Flipper'.

Lister, Dave (Third Technician)
"Amazon Women On Heat" - the cute redhead
always refuses to give me a foot massage.

     ThaT's noT a malfuncTion, you gimboid -
     jusT a sign she's noT compleTely barking insane.

Kochanski, Kristine (Navigation Officer)

  Barber of Seville A R - no way did Rossini
write a scene in which a group of drunken
Space Commandos shot up Figaro's house
because he didn't take enough off their
sideburns.

Er...that's my fault. I imported some code from
'Star Battalions' to see what would happen. Sorry!

Lister, Dave (Third Technician)
I keep trying to use the Sex-Sim A/R we found on that derelict last week but whenever I try to insert it the machine spits it out!!! Trust me to be stationed aboard the only ship in Space Corps whose A/R player suffers from premature ejection!!!

Kryten (Series 4000 Service Mechanoid)
I'm no historian but having visited the 'Great Moments in Human History' A/R several times now, I feel I have to speak out and say that I am fairly certain Torquemada did <u>not</u> speak with the voice of Donald Duck. And, if he did, then making him continually repeat the phrase 'recant thy unholy deviancy and embraceth the works of Christ thy soul's saviour' strikes me as extremely cruel (and more than slightly damp).

Okay, grunts. If you've been reading this book since the start, you now know how to survive spaceship crashes, to live on hostile worlds and to survive on less than nothing by eating bugs and grubs and, failing that, yourself. But any old survival manual will tell you that. Now it's time to get down to the nitty gritty. The REAL reason you bought this book!

At last! Fashion tips!

Here it is then, the Mike Mad Dog O'Hagan survival speciality:

SURVIVING DEATH

We demonstrate one of the more underrated survival skills "synchronized panicking"

Many people think that death is the end. That you only live once. These people are mistaken, misguided and – in most cases – moronic. Some people even go so far as to say that you should live each day as if it's your last.

WHAT A BUNCH OF PILLOCKS!

By saying this to yourself, you're actually admitting that there will be a 'last'. That every day death is moving in on you, till eventually it's closer than an anorexic's belt loops. WRONG! You can only survive if you have a positive mental attitude; you can only have a positive mental attitude if your mind is narrower than the Pope's rap collection. Your mind must not admit even the slightest possiblility of death, and your mind will only completely refuse to accept death if it can be sure that death is a survivable situation.

WHICH IT IS

OK – I'M INTERESTED; HOW DO I SURVIVE DEATH?

I'm glad you asked me that. Basically there are two ways you can go about surviving death:

1. ASSUME THE CATHOLICS ARE RIGHT

According to them (and a surprising number of religions, actually, who all seem to have plagiarised each others' ideas – it's a copyright minefield) death is not the end. When you die, so they say, your essence, which they call the 'soul', floats out of your body and sort of wafts upward to sit on a cloud and bang a tambourine all day to the tune of 'Kum ba ya'.

This is a perfectly sweet theory as far as it goes. However to the gimlet eyes of the trained Space Corps Commando there are several basic flaws, to wit:

- while the soul survives and, indeed prospers, becoming a practiced percussionist and knowing all the words to the collected works of Ralph McTell, the body withers and dies – and with it dies your ability to use semi-automatic weapons, concussion grenades, bayonets...frankly, ALL the fun stuff.

- your soul is a WUSS. Sorry but it is. You might be a fearsome and ruthless fighting machine, feared across 18 planets, but I guarantee your soul is a big girly creampuff that is moved to tears at the sight of fluffy animals and never touches hamburgers because it 'has a really really big conscience problem with factory farming'.

So stick to this method of surviving death and all you've got to look forward to is an eternity of wandering round saying you think that you shall never see a thing as lovely as a tree, when we all know a tree is only lovely when it's at one end of a high tension wire you've set up to decapitate an enemy motorcyclist.

If I were you I'd forget about religion completely.

No good can come of it and the food's awful: last Catholic do I went to they only served cheap plonk and wafers – with no ice cream!!! Who needs it?

Let us turn, gratefully, to our other method of surviving death:

2. THE SCIENTIFIC APPROACH

For at least a century scientists have been noticing that the amount of preservatives in the foods we eat has been having a significant effect on our bodies. Absorbed via the blood, these preservatives linger in our own cells, having the same effect on us as they did on food. Corpses not only take longer to decompose but look tasty and appetizing for much longer than they ever did before.

This 'preservative effect' went so far that in 2123, a coroner performing an autopsy noted that all of the subjects organs had generated their own shrink wrapping.

It was after this that a group of top scientists, led by my Uncle Max and his lab assistant Chantelle, first advanced the theory that using the latest in preservative and regenerative drugs, death could be made a survivable condition. In lab animals and, later, in my Auntie Enid, they created a state beyond death which he christened 'undeath'...a sort of not dead/not alive state which is normally only attained by 'Little Chef' waitresses.

THIS IS HOW IT WORKS

As part of your standard kit, you carry round an 'emergency death pack' of drugs, hypos, preservatives and compounds. This death pack may swell your survival kit slightly, as it weighs 11 stone (11 and a half if you go with the one that includes the 'Mine's A Stiff One!!!' T-shirts and matching baseball caps). The idea is that when you die you (or, more practically, a friend) administer these drugs which have the effect of preserving the brain and basic motor functions of the body, and of slowing down the general decomposition process.

Now, Uncle Max would be the first to admit this system is not perfect, and several people who have tried it have been somewhat disappointed by the fact that they do actually continue to decompose, albeit at a slower rate. This involves minor inconveniences, like a fetid stench and a tendency for extremities to fall off, but nothing you can't pass off with an amusing remark in company. And remember: work continues on this problem and breakthroughs are being made all the time, the latest being the discovery that some of the worst effects of decomposition can be mitigated somewhat by scotch taping an air freshener under each armpit.

Whatever the disadvantages, surviving death has several undeniable advantages, as this comparison chart shows:

Forfeit video club membership	Can still go to cinema (actually, cinemas are good places as popcorn is one of the few things that smell worse than an undead person)
People forget to invite you to parties	Still get invited out – BUT can no longer be life of party (however, at least if you forget your handbag you can dance round your hand).
Listless. Lacking in energy. Even the simplest thing seems like too much effort.	Can't wait to get out of your grave in the morning.
Even armed combat doesn't excite you like it used to.	Armed combat takes on exciting new meaning when you can wrench own arm off and beat a man to death with it.
No one comes to call anymore.	You can scare the crap out of Jehovah's Witnesses.

ADJUSTING TO DEATH

As you can imagine, undergoing death means your body will naturally go through a few changes. It's very much like the 'change of life' only we refer to it as 'the end of life'.

You may find your sex drive diminishing, which is just as well as research shows that for some reason we don't yet understand, undead people are less sexually attractive to the opposite sex than live people. Or dobermans.

There are also some other adjustments you will have to make:

● You will, for example, find it very difficult at first to stop using phrases like "as I live and breathe".

● You'll also have to be reassuring and supportive of your friends and loved ones should they become embarrassed or distressed at accidentally saying things like 'not on your life' or 'live and let live'. If they should inadvertently let one of those sayings slip, just let out a hearty chuckle and maybe snap off an index finger and throw it at them in a joshing manner.

SPACE CORPS
SURVIVAL QUESTIONNAIRE

Name:

> Kristine Kochanski

1. In your opinion, what is the first rule of survival?

> Whatever doesn't kill you just makes you stronger (unless it bites your legs off, in which case it just makes you shorter).

2. Do you enjoy violent films or vidshows?

> No. I prefer the classics. Emily Bronte. Jane Austen. Jilly Cooper (the early, socially relevant stuff).

3. Would you kill to avoid being killed?

All Space Corps personnel are trained to kill without a second's hesitation, regret or remorse. But unfortunately, I was away that day (I pretended to be ill, but really I was on a day trip to Calais).

So though I may not be able to kill without remorse, I can hold my own fighting for the last wheel of Brie in a French hypermarket - which is pretty much the same thing.

4. Can violence ever be justified?

It can be justified intellectually, but not, I think, morally. My mum used to say that violence is the last refuge of the green humpty people.

Of course, she was a heavy prozak user by that time...

5. If you could go back in time and murder Adolf Hitler as a baby – would you?

No. Because a baby is not evil. A baby is a blank slate awaiting the world to write on it. It's only then the baby becomes a person, good or bad. Of course, in very rare cases, a baby's blank-slatedness persists long into adult life (c.f. David Lister).

6. Do you believe in censorship?

No. Unless hiding Lister's guitar is censorship, in which case – yes. ~~Absolutely.~~

7. Would you use the words agnostic/atheist/deist/satanist to describe yourself?

No.
Because I don't believe in using simplistic labels to pigeonhole people. ~~And~~ anyone who does is a drooling moron.

8. How would you describe your spiritual position?

I feel we are all connected in the great Dodecahedron of Life.

But I could be wrong.
It might be a polygon.

9. Would you describe this glass

as being half full – or half empty?

I try never to judge people.
Or crockery.

10. If there was one thing you could change to make
life better – what would it be?

I'd have come up
with a better
answer to
question 4

11. What is the purpose of existen

It has no purpose. It's essentially a
collection of meaningless abstractions,
and our attempts to order them into
some sort of framework which we can
designate as a ~~purpose~~ is nothing more
than a doomed attempt to make
desperate sense of the process
leading to our death.

~~Alternatively~~ –
it's to always wear nice shoes.

Now we come to what has probably been the hardest bit of this book to write. I've started several times, but my fingers have choked with emotion on the keyboard and it's only after several hours of kickboxing that I have felt able to come back and start afresh. Here goes:

Like all other good things in life, every survival situation must, sadly, come to an end. And it's my tragic duty to remind you of this moment when your spartan idyll is over and it's back to the boring benefits of civilization, public transport and air-kissing people that 2 days ago you'd have cut down like dogs. I refer, of course, to:

RESCUE

No matter how long you put it off, you will eventually need to be rescued. Perhaps you have a party to attend, a wedding to be Best Man at, or, like me, you're a fixture in the annual Space Corps Tai Kwan Do tournament. It's a son of a bitch – but it's time to call in the cavalry.

HOW DO I GET RESCUED?

Good question. Well, assuming they even know you are missing (or care) your ship or space station will doubtless have sent a team out to find you. Here are some of the most effective ways of attracting the attention of manned or unmanned rescue probes:

GROUND TO SATELLITE SIGNALS

Need food and water

Am travelling this way

Safe to land here

Children under 13 not
admitted to this planet unless
accompanied by an adult

We are very bored

Have crap sense of humour

Have been crushed
to death by a falling
meteorite

BODY SIGNALS

The following diagram illustrates a series of signals which will be understood by any space crews who might be searching for you. Whenever you are making signals make sure all your movements are very visible and extremely exaggerated.

Can ~~proceed shortly~~
HELP!
My sweater is too long...

Need ~~mechanical~~ help
I am stupendously well endowed

~~Everything OK~~
Damn! Got the hairspray
mixed up with the underarm
deodorant AGAIN!!!

~~Land here~~
Warning!
French Toilet

SPACE CORPS SURVIVAL MANUAL

~~Our radio is working~~
Rimmer organ recital
night Tonight!!!

~~Do not attempt to land here~~
Scottish Goalkeeper

~~Drop a message~~
My nail varnish is wet

Yes
I have a kleenex and I'm
not afraid to use it!

~~Need URGENT medical help~~
Great party last night.

Have Anti-Gravity
Device

CONCLUSION

And that's it. You've reached the end of this manual. Whaddya want – a MEDAL? Well, you got something better than that, soldier. You've now got a working knowledge of how to survive some of the toughest conditions in the universe — including death itself! So you now have NO EXCUSES! When you go down on a hostile planet, whether you live or whether you die – WE EXPECT YOU BACK AT WORK by the following Monday. Dismissed!!!

Mike

Publisher's note: subsequent to the writing of this conclusion, Colonel O'Hagan disappeared without a trace when his ship went down over Tregar IV. The other survivors of the crash ate Colonel O'Hagan using one of his own delicious recipes and used the manuscript pages of this book to insulate their igloo. Certain sections of the book were also eaten and we look forward to bringing them to you as 'The Star Corps Survival Manual II – This Time It's Personal' as soon as the laxatives take effect.

OFFICIAL RED DWARF FAN CLUBS:

UK: 40 Pitford Road, Woodley, Reading, Berks RG5 4QF
Ireland: 67 Rafters Road, Drimnagh, Dublin 12, Ireland
Australia: PO Box 1044, Bundoora, Victoria 3083, Australia
USA: PO Box 13097, Coyote, CA 95013, USA

VIDEO

Series 1-6, plus SMEG UPS and SMEG OUTS are available from
BBC Video. Mail order hotline: 0181 576 2000.

BOOKS

Four Red Dwarf novels (*Infinity Welcomes Careful Drivers*,
Better than Life, *Last Human* and *Backwards*) are available from
Penguin (mail order: 0181 899 4036) and also as audiobooks from
Laughing Stock (0181 944 9455) and Polygram (0181 910 5000).
Other books are *The Official Companion* (Titan: 01536 763631);
The Making of Red Dwarf (Penguin); *The Quiz Book* (Penguin);
The Programme Guide (Virgin: 0181 968 7554) and *The Man
Behind the Rubber Mask* (Penguin).

CLOTHING AND ACCESSORIES

Jackets, sweatshirts, t-shirts, baseball caps and mugs are available
from Distribution Network (mail order: 0181 543 1231); pewter
badges and dogtags from Alchemy Carta (0116 2824824).

A range of Red Dwarf posters and calendars (Scandecor:
0171 371 5274), greetings cards (Portico Designs (0117 9478870)
and model kits (Sevan Models: 01225 777110) are also available.